This book belongs to

MY BIG BEAR STORYBOOK

Illustrations by Rebecca Archer

Stories by Kath Mellentin and Tim Wood

OYSTER BOOKS

YELLOW BEAR'S BIG CRASH

TING! TING! TING!

Tiny Bear rang her bicycle bell loudly.

"Race you round the garden," she shouted to Small Bear. And off they went, down the path.

The race was a dead heat!

Just then, Yellow Bear appeared, pushing a shiny red bicycle.

"Why aren't you riding your new bike?" asked Grey Bear.

"I've never ridden a two-wheeler before," said Yellow Bear, nervously.

"It's easy," called Orange Bear. "Follow me."

Yellow Bear pedalled off after Orange Bear. At first, things went well. But as Yellow Bear got near the end of the garden, her bike started to wobble. She knew she ought to use her brakes to slow down, and turn her handlebars to steer round the vegetable patch. But she couldn't decide which to do first! She got so flustered, she completely forgot to watch where she was going.

"Look out!" shouted Big Bear.

"Help!" spluttered Yellow Bear as her bike tipped over and she fell with a thump on to the grass.

The Bears rushed over.

"Are you all right?" asked Grey Bear.

"I've bumped my knee," sniffed Yellow Bear, bravely, wiping a tear from her eye.

Tiny Bear fetched some sticking plaster and put it on Yellow Bear's bump.

"You'll soon feel better," soothed Panda Bear.

"Let's all help Yellow Bear learn to ride,"
suggested Black Bear.

"I'll lend you my cycling helmet," said White Bear,
kindly, undoing the chin strap.

"And you can borrow my knee pads and elbow
guards," added Grey Bear.

Yellow Bear was soon ready.

"Now then," said Black Bear. "I'll hold the bike
steady while you get on."

"I think your saddle is too high," said Grey Bear. "Just wait while I get a spanner."

Grey Bear went to the garden shed and fetched a spanner. She undid a nut and lowered the saddle.

"Try that," she said.

"That's much better, thank you," said Yellow Bear.

"I'll hold you steady while you cycle round," promised Big Bear.

"Don't try to go too fast," advised Brown Bear.

Soon Yellow Bear was cycling happily round the garden. Big Bear trotted behind, holding the saddle. Then, when Yellow Bear wasn't looking, he let go!

Yellow Bear wobbled a bit, then gently squeezed the brakes, steered round the vegetable patch and cycled up the path.

"It's easy!" she called. "I can ride by myself."

The Bears cheered. "Hooray for Bicycle Bear!"

BATH TIME FOR ORANGE BEAR

SPLISH! SPLASH! SPLOSH!

Orange Bear was playing his favourite game - jumping in muddy puddles.

"You'll get so dirty," scolded Big Bear. "You haven't even got your wellies on!"

"Wheee!" shouted Orange Bear, jumping into another puddle. "I don't care! I like being dirty!"

"Watch out, Orange Bear!" complained White Bear. "You're splashing mud everywhere."

"I don't care," laughed Orange Bear. "I like being muddy!"

"It's tea time," called Panda Bear.

Orange Bear skipped up the path.

The Bears gasped when they saw him.

"You are MUCH too dirty to sit down and eat,"
said Yellow Bear. "You'll have to wash your hands."

"... and your face," said Grey Bear.

"... and your feet," said Brown Bear.

"... in fact, all of you," said Tiny Bear, firmly.

"You need a bath," said Big Bear.

"I HATE baths," said Orange Bear.

"Baths are FUN, if you use my bubble bath," said Yellow Bear.

"...and play with my toy boat," said Small Bear.

"...and my rubber shark," said Black Bear.

"...and my blow-up alligator," added Brown Bear.

"...and my squirting octopus," smiled Grey Bear.

KERSPLOSH!

Orange Bear jumped into the soapy water.

"This is nearly as much fun as jumping in muddy puddles!" he cried.

In no time at all, Orange Bear was as clean as clean as a Bear can be.

"I feel much better now," said Orange Bear, brushing crumbs from his whiskers. "It's quite nice to be clean!"

"You look much better, too," laughed Big Bear. "You're orange again, instead of muddy brown!"

"But the BEST thing about being clean ...," said Orange Bear just five minutes later, ... "is getting DIRTY again!"

SPLAT!

PANDA BEAR'S SURPRISE VISITOR

RAT-A-TAT-TAT!

Someone was knocking at the door.

"It's my Great Uncle Panda!" cried Panda Bear. "He's back!"

Great Uncle Panda was a famous explorer. He had been away on an expedition for a whole year.

"Hello there, Bears," boomed Great Uncle Panda. "I've come to stay."

"But we don't have a spare bedroom," said White Bear, in a worried voice.

"Explorers don't need bedrooms," chuckled Great Uncle Panda. "I'll sleep in my tent."

The Bears helped Great Uncle Panda put up his tent. Then they piled all his bags, trunks and boxes into a huge mountain.

"Let's go in for tea now," squeaked Tiny Bear.

"Explorers don't eat indoors," chortled Great Uncle Panda. "They cook their food on campfires."

"Let's have our very own campfire!" said the Bears, excitedly.

Great Uncle Panda took charge and the Bears were soon sitting comfortably in the warm glow.

The Bears sat for hours around the campfire, open-mouthed and wide-eyed as Great Uncle Panda told them all about his adventures. There were stories of lions, tigers, thundering waterfalls and exploding volcanoes. Finally, darkness fell. Great Uncle Panda paused.

"That's enough for tonight," he smiled. "It's long past bedtime. We explorers have to get up at dawn, you know, so we never stay up too late."

"Goodnight," murmured the Bears, sleepily.

"I hope Great Uncle Panda will tell us more stories today," said Black Bear next morning.

But Great Uncle Panda was nowhere to be seen. The tent and the mountain of bags, trunks and boxes had vanished, too.

"What's happened?" asked Brown Bear.

"He's gone," said Yellow Bear. "Look. He's left a note."

"Never mind," said Tiny Bear. "Let's build a pretend campfire of our own and play at being explorers."

And that is exactly what they did.

All that talk about expeditions has made me want to go exploring again. I'm off to the Arctic to visit the Polar Bears. See you next year.

Love
G.U.P.

GOODNIGHT, SMALL BEAR

THUMP! THUMP!

Up the stairs went the Bears, one by one. It was time for bed. They washed their faces and paws, brushed their teeth and put on their pyjamas.

"May we have a bedtime story, please?" asked White Bear.

While Small Bear read their favourite story, *Goldilocks*, the Bears snuggled under the covers.

"Goodnight, everyone," said Small Bear when the story was over.

"Goodnight, Small Bear," replied the others.

CRASH! BANG! WALLOP!

The Bears sat up with a start.

"What was that?" squeaked Tiny Bear.

"It's only thunder!" soothed Small Bear. "Don't be frightened. I'll come and tuck you in."

Small Bear jumped out of bed and tucked the covers snugly round Tiny Bear.

"I'm thirsty!" called Orange Bear. "May I have a drink
of water?"

"May I have one, too?" asked Brown Bear.
CRASH! went the thunder.

"I'll get you some water when the storm is over,"
replied Big Bear, nervously.

"I'm not afraid of silly old thunder,"
said Small Bear, bravely.
He jumped out of bed
and went downstairs.
He was soon back with
two glasses of water.

"Here you are," he smiled.

"I'm hungry!" called Yellow Bear. FLASH! went
the lightning.

"I'll get you a biscuit when the storm is over,"
replied Big Bear, nervously.

"I'm not afraid of silly old lightning," said Small
Bear, bravely. He jumped out of bed and went
downstairs. He was soon back with a biscuit.

"Here you are," he smiled.

"Who's tapping on the window?" whispered Black
Bear. "And what's that shadow on the wall?"

WHOOSH! went the wind.

"I don't know," growled Big Bear, nervously.

"It's just the wind in the trees and the moonlight
shining through the window," said Small Bear. "I'll
draw the curtains tight shut, and then you won't be
frightened."

At last the thunder stopped and the storm died down.
The Bears didn't feel frightened any more.

"Thank you, Small Bear," said Big Bear. "We think
you're ever so brave."

But Small Bear said nothing. Helping the other
Bears had tired him out. He was fast asleep.

"Goodnight, Small Bear."

BIG BEAR'S BIRTHDAY

CLANG!

Big Bear closed the front gate and trotted up the garden path. Today was his birthday.

"Hello!" he called. But there was no reply.

"That's funny," he thought. "Where is everybody?" Big Bear looked into the play room. Tiny Bear and Small Bear were playing on the climbing frame.

"Hello, Big Bear," they called.

"Hello," replied Big Bear. "Er, do you know what day it is?"

"Tuesday," said Small Bear, hanging upside down.

"Perhaps they've forgotten it's my birthday," thought Big Bear, walking towards the kitchen. But when he tried to open the door, he found it was stuck.

"No," he thought, turning the handle again. "It's not stuck. It's locked."

He tapped on the door. "What do you want?" called White Bear from inside.

"Let me in," called Big Bear.

"Go away," replied White Bear. "I'm busy cooking."

Big Bear went towards the living room. But Orange
Bear stood in the way.

"You can't come in here, Big Bear," said Orange
Bear. "We're busy tidying up."

"I'm not having a very friendly birthday," thought
Big Bear, wandering into the garden. "Perhaps
Yellow Bear will talk to me."

But Yellow Bear ran past carrying a big box, then rushed behind the garden shed.

"Do you want to play, Yellow Bear?" called Big Bear.

"Er - no," replied Yellow Bear. "I can't, sorry. I'm much too busy."

"Well, can I help then?" asked Big Bear.

"That's very kind," replied Yellow Bear. "But I've nearly finished."

Big Bear sat down on the grass.

"What a rotten birthday," he sighed. "Everyone is too busy to talk to me or play with me."

Just then, everything went dark.

"What's happening?" asked Big Bear, startled.

Then he realised that someone's paws had covered his eyes. Another bear took hold of his arm and led him into the house.

When the paws were pulled away, Big Bear was in the living room. And it had been laid out for a party!

"I thought you had all forgotten," said Big Bear.

"Of course we hadn't forgotten," smiled White Bear. "But we didn't want you to see your birthday cake, or the decorations!"

"Or the hiding places for your birthday treasure hunt," added Yellow Bear.

"Silly me," laughed Big Bear.

White Bear brought in Big Bear's cake, and the Bears all sang "Happy Birthday". Big Bear had the best birthday ever.

WHITE BEAR'S SNOWY DAY

BRINNNNG!

The alarm clock rang loudly. White Bear
jumped out of bed and ran to the window. She
drew the curtains and clapped her paws in delight.

"Hooray!" she cheered. "It's snowing! Get up,
sleepyheads! Let's go outside and build a snow bear."

Tiny Bear and Small Bear got out of bed.

"It does look pretty," said Tiny Bear, peering
through the frosty glass.

"But it feels ever so cold," said Small Bear,
shivering.

"I like summer, when the weather is hot," announced Orange Bear.

"Winter is too cold for bears," added Brown Bear.

"Wake me up when it's spring," growled Black Bear.

Panda Bear peeped out then snuggled down again.

Big Bear just snored.

White Bear went to make breakfast. Soon the delicious smell of freshly-made honey cakes wafted up the stairs. One by one, the Bears' noses began to twitch. One by one, they got up, washed and dressed. One by one, they came downstairs. Soon they were all sitting round the table.

White Bear put on her warmest clothes and ran outside.

"Come and play," she called, throwing snowballs at the kitchen window. "We'll have a snowball fight!"

The Bears looked at each other.

"It does look fun," said Yellow Bear....

Soon all the Bears were in the garden. They threw
snowballs. They pulled each other round the garden
on a sledge. They built an enormous snow bear.
They had such a good time!

When their noses and paws began to tingle
with cold, the Bears decided to go indoors. Big Bear
dished out bowls of hot soup, and the Bears were
soon warm and cosy again.

"I liked playing in the snow," said Orange Bear.

"I liked the snowball fight," said Tiny Bear.

"I liked sledging," said Black Bear.

"We liked making the snow bear," said Brown Bear and Grey Bear.

"I do hope it snows again tonight," said Panda Bear, gazing at the starry sky.

White Bear said nothing. She just smiled.

BLACK BEAR'S SPOTTY DAY

SCRATCH! SCRATCH! SCRATCH!

Black Bear woke up one morning feeling very itchy.

"I feel rather strange," he thought, as he went into the bathroom to clean his teeth.

Black Bear looked in the mirror and jumped in surprise.

"Oh, dear!" he exclaimed. "My face is all spotty."

"I think you had better go back to bed," said Big Bear, anxiously. "You're spotty all over!"

"I'll call the doctor," said White Bear.

White Bear bustled into the bedroom.

"The doctor can't come round until this afternoon," she announced.

"You'll have to stay in bed," said Grey Bear.

"Oh, no!" groaned Black Bear. "I wanted to go rollerblading."

"Don't worry, we'll stay with you and play some games," offered Yellow Bear, cheerily.

They played ...

Counting Black Bear's Spots...

I Spy With My Little Eye...

and Puppet Theatres....

Orange Bear plumped up the pillows.

Brown Bear brought a bowl of hot soup.

Panda Bear brought a cool flannel to wipe
Black Bear's face.

The Bears kept Black Bear so busy, he had
no time to feel itchy.

Just after lunch, the doctor arrived. She gently
shooed all the Bears out of the room.

"Say 'Ah'," she told Black Bear.

"Ah!" said Black Bear.

The doctor put a big thermometer into Black
Bear's mouth and took his temperature.

"Do your spots itch?" she asked.

"Mmmmm!" mumbled Black Bear, nodding.

"I'm not surprised," smiled the doctor. "You've
got chicken pox."

"Black Bear has chicken pox," the doctor explained. "I was going to tell you all not to get too close to him, but I can see it's too late."

"What do you mean?" squeaked Small Bear.

"Look at yourselves," said the doctor.

The Bears stared at each other. They were all just as spotty as Black Bear!

"Whatever shall we do?" asked White Bear.

The doctor gave the Bears a huge bottle of pink lotion to stop the spots itching and told them all to stay indoors for a week.

"We can take it in turns to look after each other," said Brown Bear. "And we don't have to worry any more about Black Bear feeling lonely!"

Black Bear, who had been looking very glum, cheered up at once. Perhaps having chicken pox wasn't going to be so bad after all.

TINY BEAR'S FIRST DAY AT SCHOOL

CLANG! CLANG!

"That's the school bell," said Grey Bear.

Tiny Bear looked up nervously. Today was her first day at play school.

"Is it time to go already?" she asked, in a wobbly voice.

"Yes," replied Big Bear, cheerfully. "Hurry up."

"I can't find my satchel," whispered Tiny Bear.

Panda Bear pulled out a shiny new satchel from behind the sofa. Tiny Bear's ears turned pink.

"I must have left it there last night," she said, in a small voice.

The Bears walked briskly up the hill and across
the fields to play school. Tiny Bear dawdled behind.

"Don't be nervous," said Brown Bear. "Play
school is great fun."

Miss Honey, the teacher, welcomed them.

"Hello, Tiny Bear," she beamed.

Tiny Bear was busy all morning. She played in the sand pit, painted pictures, and learnt how to skip. She was so busy, she forgot to be nervous.

At story time, Tiny Bear sat beside White Bear. They listened to a tale about a castle, a dragon and brave Sir Bear. Tiny Bear thought it was the best story she had ever heard.

When the school bell rang, Tiny Bear looked disappointed. "Is it time to go already?" she asked.

Tiny Bear skipped all the way home.

"I like play school!" she sang.

"What was the best thing about play school?"
asked Black Bear, when they were eating their tea.

"The sandpit?" asked Big Bear.

"The story?" asked Brown Bear.

"The painting?" asked Grey Bear.

"No," laughed Tiny Bear, after she had thought
for a while. "The best thing about play school is that
you are all there to look after me."

BROWN BEAR'S VOYAGE

SPER-LOOSH! SPER-LOOSH!

Yellow Bear and Tiny Bear were paddling in the sea. Water was splashing everywhere!

"Watch out, you two!" called Panda Bear. "You'll wash my sandcastle away."

The Bears were at the seaside. They were having a wonderful time. Panda Bear was building the biggest sandcastle in the world. Big Bear and Small Bear were eating ice-creams. Black Bear and Grey Bear were exploring a mysterious rock pool.

"We've caught a giant crab!" shouted Grey Bear.

Just then, a little boat sailed past.

"Ahoy there!" called Captain Brown Bear.

"Heave ho, my hearties!" First Mate White Bear saluted like a real sailor.

The Bears all waved like mad.

As the little boat passed the jetty, Old Sailor Bear called out.

"Will you take a parcel to the lighthouse?" he asked.

"Aye aye sir!" replied Brown Bear, smartly.

"Ahoy there!" Lighthouse Bear greeted the sailors when they arrived.

"We've brought a parcel for you," announced Brown Bear. "It's food from Old Sailor Bear."

"Why, thank you," smiled Lighthouse Bear. "That's my breakfasts, lunches and dinners for a whole week."

"Don't you get lonely working here all by yourself?" asked Brown Bear.

"Why, no!" laughed Lighthouse Bear. "I've got Polly for company. Come in and I'll introduce you."

The steep, winding staircase led to the strangest room the Bears had ever seen. It was completely round. The walls were all glass and in the middle was a giant light.

"I turn the light on when it gets dark," explained Lighthouse Bear. "It turns round and round. The light flashes across the sea and warns ships to keep away from the rocks."

"Turn on the light!" squawked a voice.

"Meet Polly, my parrot," laughed Lighthouse Bear.

"Time for tea! Time for tea!" squawked Polly.

After tea, the Bears explored the lighthouse.

There were lots of little rooms - all of them round.

"Bring your friends to visit tomorrow," said

Lighthouse Bear, as the Bears got ready to leave.

"Squawk!" said Polly.

Brown Bear steered the little boat carefully back to the shore. The other Bears ran to greet the two sailors.

"We've been on a mystery voyage!" announced Captain Brown Bear, importantly.

"Gather round and we'll tell you all about our adventures," added White Bear. "And if you're very good, we'll take you on your very own mystery voyage tomorrow!"

GREY BEAR'S CIRCUS

ZZZZ! ZZZZ! ZZZZ!

It was a lazy Sunday afternoon. The Bears were snoozing in the play room. Grey Bear was reading.

"Wake up, everyone," she called all of a sudden. "Come and look at this wonderful picture of a circus."

The other Bears crowded round. They all admired the picture Grey Bear had found showing a huge circus tent full of acrobats, jugglers, fire eaters and trapeze artists.

"Let's play circuses," suggested Grey Bear.

"Oh, yes, let's!" agreed the Bears.

"I'll be the ring master," squeaked Tiny Bear.
"I'll be a juggler," said Orange Bear.
"We'll be acrobats," chorused Brown Bear, Small Bear and Yellow Bear.
"I'll be the strong man," announced Big Bear.
"We'll be trick cyclists," said Panda Bear and Black Bear.
"And I'll play the circus music," cried White Bear.
But Grey Bear said nothing.

After lunch the fun began.
"My Lords, Ladies and Gentle
Bears," squeaked Tiny Bear.
"Welcome to the Grand Bear Circus!"
White Bear rolled the drums and,
one by one, the Bears
performed their acts.
Orange Bear juggled, the
trick cyclists raced round and
round, and Big Bear flexed his
muscles. The

acrobats
turned
somersaults
and cartwheels then made
a sort of wobbly Bear
pyramid which soon fell
down in a giggling heap.

"And now the final act," squeaked Tiny Bear. "Greybo the clown!"

Grey Bear rushed into the ring. The Bears gasped at her wonderful clown costume with floppy bow tie and baggy trousers. She had used face paints to make a clown face and a kitchen mop to make a wig. She had even made giant cardboard shoes.

The Bears roared with laughter as Grey Bear did her tricks. She tripped over her long shoes. She put

her foot in a bucket of water. Finally she took out a custard pie and pretended to throw it at the Bears. They all ducked, and then howled with laughter when Grey Bear threw the pie at herself!

Finally the circus was over. All the performers bowed in turn and the audience clapped and cheered.

"Hooray for the Circus Bears!"

But the biggest cheer and the loudest clap of all was when Grey Bear took her bow.